# Super Fun Reading Comprehension Activity Workbook

Comprehension strategies are used to increase children's understanding of the text to help them become active readers. It requires the ability to make inferences from a passage and use critical thinking skills to answer questions related to the text.

Wonder House

# 1 HELPING HARRY

Sally was sitting on the couch, watching television. Her mom walked in the door with Harry, their dog. Harry walked right over to Sally and licked her hello. "Hi Harry! How was your checkup?" Sally asked. Harry just looked at Sally. "We have to help Harry," said Mom. "Help her how?" asked Sally. "Do you remember when we went to pick up Harry from her litter? We picked her because she looked like her mom. She was brown with spots, with long ears, and she was energetic, so we thought she'd be strong, like her mom. But how does she look now?" Mom asked. "Well," thought Sally, "She's still brown with spots and long ears, but she's not very energetic or strong anymore." "That's what the vet said, too. We haven't been letting her exercise as much, and we've been feeding her a lot. She would probably look just like her mom if we had walked her more. We have to start walking her more often, so that she'll stay healthy for a long time. Will you help?" "Sure!" said Sally.

She decided that she could play fetch with her every day in the yard, because then she could run and run and run until she was tired. The first day, they only played fetch for about 10 minutes before Harry was tired. But Sally kept playing with her every day. Soon, they could play for an entire half an hour! Harry looked stronger every day, just like her mom. Sally felt great about helping Harry get strong again.

## a. Answer the questions.

1. What was Sally doing when her mom walked in?

   ---------------------------------------------

2. Where did mom take Harry and why?

   ---------------------------------------------

3. How did Harry appear when it was a puppy?

   ---------------------------------------------

4. What did Sally's mom suggest to make Harry strong?

   ---------------------------------------------

5. What did Sally do to make Harry fit and strong?

   ---------------------------------------------

## b. What are the young ones of these animals?

| Animal | Young Ones | | | |
|---|---|---|---|---|
| Pig | a. Piglet | b. Foal | c. Kit | d. None of these |
| Lion | a. Calf | b. Cub | c. Lamb | d. Pup |
| Deer | a. Fawn | b. Lamb | c. Cub | d. Colt |
| Cow | a. Pup | b. Cub | c. Cygnet | d. Calf |
| Dog | a. Kitten | b. Puppy | c. Foal | d. None of these |

c. Make 10 words by unscrambling the letters in the word TELEVISION.

---

---

---

---

d. Write singular and plural words in the correct column.

foot child ox woman men tooth goose teeth
person cacti oxen children man people feet
geese cactus women

| Singular | Plural |
| --- | --- |
| | |
| | |
| | |
| | |
| | |

# THE LIFE CYCLE

2

When you plant a seed, does it stay a seed forever? No! Plants and animals grow and change throughout their lives. Many plants begin as seeds. As the seed gets what it needs (water, sunlight, and nutrients from the soil), it begins to germinate. The seed turns into a little sprout called seedling. It keeps growing until it is a full-grown plant. Then the plant makes new seeds, so that new plants can grow. Because seeds go through this process over and over again, it is called a life cycle.

Animals also have life cycles. A frog begins as an egg. When the egg hatches, it turns into a tadpole. The tadpoles grow legs and arms, and eventually grow into adult frogs. The adult frogs lay eggs, so that new frogs can live even after the frog grows old and dies. A dog's life cycle is a little different than a frog's, because a dog does not start out as an egg, but mama dog gives birth to her young ones.

Insects like caterpillars go through life cycles, too. Caterpillars begin as eggs. When they hatch, they are larva. The caterpillar becomes a pupa, and inside the pupa it turns into an adult. The adult is not a caterpillar; it is a butterfly! Then the butterfly lays eggs, so that new caterpillars and butterflies can live even after the butterfly grows old and dies. Living organisms don't stay the same throughout their lives, they grow and change through their life cycle.

**a. Answer the following questions.**

1. What is the first stage in the life of a plant?

_______________________________________________

2. What does a seed require to grow into a plant?

_______________________________________________

3. Define life cycle.

_______________________________________________

4. How is a dog's life cycle different from a frog?

_______________________________________________

5. What are the various stages in the life cycle of a butterfly?

_______________________________________________

**b. Find the correct word in the passage for each phrase.**

1. a living thing ______________________________
2. the stages of life ______________________________
3. to make offspring ______________________________
4. to begin to grow ______________________________
5. a young plant ______________________________

**c. Arrange the stages in the right order.**

| Life Cycle of a Frog | Stage |
|---|---|
| eggs | |
| tadpole with legs and arms | |
| tadpole | |
| adult frog | |
| froglet | |

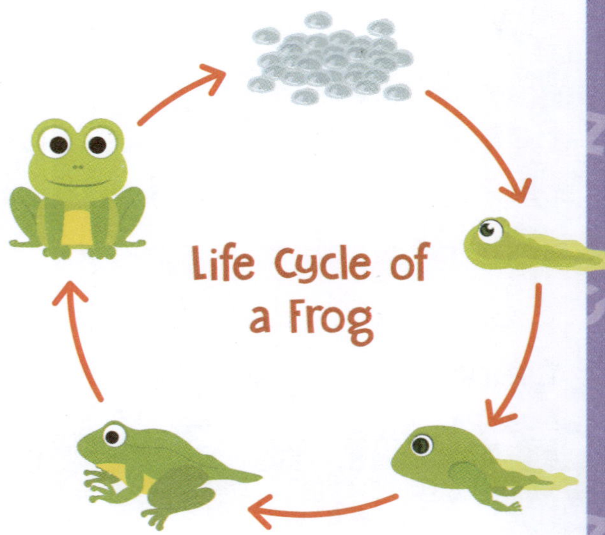


**d. Fill in the blanks.**

1. Seeds go through a process over and over again, it is called a __________.

2. A frog begins as an __________. When the egg hatches, it turns into a tadpole.

3. Mama dog gives birth to her __________.

4. A seed needs water, __________ and __________ from the soil.

5. Caterpillars begin as eggs. When they hatch, they are called __________.

# 3 THE LITTLE ARCHITECTS

Bees live in a house that is called a hive. There are three kinds of bees: workers, drones, and queens. Only one queen bee can live in each hive. If she is lost or dead, the other bees will stop their work. They will appoint another bee as their queen and then start to work under her supervision.

In winters, the worker bees crowd around the queen bee in the center of the hive to keep her warm. They change places frequently within the hive, so all may stay warm. They eat their honey to keep themselves warm. Honey bees get all their nutrition from pollen and nectar. In summers, worker bees will collect water from streams and ponds to cool the hive.

Bees are very wise and busy little creatures. They all join together to build cells of wax for their honey. Each bee takes its proper place and does its own work. Some go out and gather honey from the flowers; others stay at home and work inside the hive. The cells which they build are all of one shape and size, and no room is left between them. The cells are not round. They have six sides. Did you ever look into a glass hive to see the bees while at work? It is pleasant to see how busy they always are. But the drones do not work. Before winter comes, all the drones are driven from the hive so that they don't eat the honey which they did not gather.

It is not safe for children to handle bees. Bees have a painful sting that they use in their defense. Bees communicate by means of dances and emitting sounds.

## a. Answer the questions.

1. Where do bees live?

_______________________________________________

2. What are the three kinds of bees?

_______________________________________________

3. How do bees communicate?

_______________________________________________

4. Describe a beehive.

_______________________________________________

5. Who are more active, the drones or the workers?

_______________________________________________

## b. Write three words that rhyme.

1. honey _______________________________________________
2. team _______________________________________________
3. wax _______________________________________________
4. plan _______________________________________________
5. cell _______________________________________________

c. Find the words in the box.

BEE CELL WAX HONEY DRONES NECTAR

HIVE DANCE STING QUEEN

| W | A | X | D | L | E | Q | U | E | E | N | D |
|---|---|---|---|---|---|---|---|---|---|---|---|
| I | I | J | A | Y | P | D | U | C | L | I | R |
| T | T | D | H | O | N | E | Y | S | E | O | O |
| E | O | R | S | H | E | L | L | P | B | W | N |
| S | L | I | I | B | I | A | R | S | N | Q | E |
| E | U | H | N | E | C | T | A | R | S | G | S |
| V | N | M | O | N | C | E | L | L | S | N | A |
| D | A | N | C | E | E | S | O | S | A | I | S |
| E | H | A | Z | K | U | M | L | Y | R | T | F |
| V | B | E | E | N | C | H | E | S | G | S | I |
| I | I | M | I | T | A | T | O | R | S | T | N |
| H | E | A | B | E | L | L | A | M | E | Y | C |

d. It's time to make sentences!

1. defense ______________________

2. pleasant ______________________

3. creature ______________________

4. supervise ______________________

5. communicate ______________________

# THE RAT AND THE CRAB

**4**

Once upon a time there was a rat and a crab. They were great friends. One day they went to the forest to get firewood. As they were going through the woods enjoying each other's company, they came across a papaya tree with a fruit that seemed too good to ignore. They stopped and debated over who will climb up and get it.

To decide who is going to climb up, they devised a way. Each of them were to collect ten twigs of varying sizes and whosoever brings it first will climb the tree. So both of them went ahead and crab brought the twigs first. So, the crab went up but half way up he broke off one of his legs and so he climbed back down. Then rat climbed all the way up and reached the fruit and started eating it.

The crab was waiting on the ground and asked him, "Aren't you going to share the fruit with me?" The rat didn't respond and kept eating. The crab then left the rat and went his way.

While walking beside the stream he saw a fish, a big red snapper fish. He caught the fish and brought it to eat. While he was eating the fish, the rat caught up to him and saw him with the red snapper fish and said, "That looks delicious." The crab said to him, "Even though you didn't share, I would still share mine if you promise to share whatever you have." They agreed on it and left together with a delicious meal waiting to be eaten.

## a. Answer the following questions.

1. Where were the friends going?

___________________________________________

2. What did the rat and crab see in the forest?

___________________________________________

3. Why couldn't the crab get his hands on the fruit?

___________________________________________

4. What promise did the rat make to the crab?

___________________________________________

5. Suggest a different title for the passage.

___________________________________________

## b. Fill in the blanks with the correct form of the verb.

1. The rat __________ (climb) all the way up and reached the fruit.

2. The rat didn't __________ (respond) and kept eating.

3. They agreed on it and __________ (leave) together.

4. "That __________ (look) delicious," said the rat.

5. One day they __________ (go) to the forest to get firewood.

**c. Tick the correct option.**

1. Which sentence is most likely true?

   a) The crab and the rat quarreled to climb up the tree.

   b) They agreed to climb together.

   c) They debated over who will climb up.

2. Which sentence is most unlikely?

   a) The rat climbed all the way up.

   b) The rat climbed all the way up and started eating the fruit.

   c) The crab climbed up and threw the fruit on the ground.

3. In this passage, the phrase too good to ignore means

   a) bad

   b) unworthy

   c) a must try

**d. Fill the crossword using clues.**

Across

1. The crab saw a ________ while walking beside the stream.

4. The crab caught a big red snapper from the _________.

Down

1. Both crab and rat went to the _________ to get firewoods.

2. _________ broke its leg while climbing up the tree.

3. The crab was waiting on the ________.

# 5 THE ELEPHANTS AND THE MICE

There was a village that was abandoned by its people after it shattered, post an earthquake. However, the mice living in the village decided to stay and make it their home.

On the outskirts of this village, there was a lake, where a herd of elephants visited regularly to bathe and drink water. Since the village was on the way to this lake, the elephants trampled the mice while walking there. The mice pleaded to their King, "Oh wise King, save us from these crazy elephants, or else they will demolish our homes. They will kill all of us!" The King guaranteed his fellow mice, "Do not get worried my dear friends, nothing will happen." So, the king of mice decided to meet the elephants. He requested them to change their route and he will remember and return the favor when they will be in need. The elephant king laughed over this and said, "Nevertheless, we honor your request and will change our route."

After a few days, the elephants got trapped and entangled in nets that were set up by hunters. They struggled hard to escape, but in vain. The elephant king remembered the promise made by the king of mice. So, he sent a fellow elephant who got lucky and was not trapped, to ask the mice king to come and help them.

Soon, all the mice came and started nibbling the nets, and freed the elephants. The elephant king couldn't thank the mice enough!

a. **Answer the questions.**

1. Why was the village abandoned by its people?

_ _ _ _ _ _ _ _ _ _ _ _ _ _ _ _ _ _ _ _ _ _ _ _ _ _ _ _ _ _ _ _ _ _ _ _ _ _ _ _ _

2. Who inhabited the village after the people left?

_ _ _ _ _ _ _ _ _ _ _ _ _ _ _ _ _ _ _ _ _ _ _ _ _ _ _ _ _ _ _ _ _ _ _ _ _ _ _ _ _

3. Where did the elephants visit regularly?

_ _ _ _ _ _ _ _ _ _ _ _ _ _ _ _ _ _ _ _ _ _ _ _ _ _ _ _ _ _ _ _ _ _ _ _ _ _ _ _ _

4. What did the mice king say to the elephant king?

_ _ _ _ _ _ _ _ _ _ _ _ _ _ _ _ _ _ _ _ _ _ _ _ _ _ _ _ _ _ _ _ _ _ _ _ _ _ _ _ _

5. What happened when elephants got trapped?

_ _ _ _ _ _ _ _ _ _ _ _ _ _ _ _ _ _ _ _ _ _ _ _ _ _ _ _ _ _ _ _ _ _ _ _ _ _ _ _ _

b. **Find the word in the passage which means the same.**

1. deserted _ _ _ _ _ _ _ _ _ _ _ _ _ _ _ _ _ _ _ _

2. adjured _ _ _ _ _ _ _ _ _ _ _ _ _ _ _ _ _ _ _ _

3. stuck _ _ _ _ _ _ _ _ _ _ _ _ _ _ _ _ _ _ _ _

4. fringes _ _ _ _ _ _ _ _ _ _ _ _ _ _ _ _ _ _ _ _

5. treaded _ _ _ _ _ _ _ _ _ _ _ _ _ _ _ _ _ _ _ _

**c. Number the phrases in the order of the story.**

Mice king went with his request. ◯

Elephants changed the route. ◯

Mice decided to make village their home. ◯

The village was hit by a catastrophic earthquake. ◯

The elephants trampled the mice while walking. ◯

The mice helped save the trapped elephants. ◯

**d. Rearrange the words to form meaningful sentences.**

1. mice / elephants / the / trampled / the / walking / while

   ---------------------------------------------

2. nets / the / got / and / entangled / in / elephants / trapped

   ---------------------------------------------

3. living / mice / the / village / decided / stay / the / in / to

   ---------------------------------------------

4. all / mice / and / nibbling / nets / the / came / the / started

   ---------------------------------------------

5. herd / and / bathe / of / a / to / drink / visited / regularly / elephants / water

   ---------------------------------------------

# MACAWS

6

The macaw is a bird that is part of the parrot family. Macaws are intelligent and curious birds that like to explore and keep busy. They are very well aware of their surroundings, which is necessary to keep watch for predators. Macaws are known for their bright colors like red, yellow, and blue. They are also known for their special talent. Macaws can mimic human speech! Macaws live in the rainforest, and they can live up to eighty years. They eat nuts, seeds, and berries, which they find in the forest. These colorful birds help the rainforest by spreading the seeds of plants as they crack open nuts, seeds, and berries.

Macaws might be small or large. Some weigh less than a pound and are shorter than twelve inches. Others can weigh several pounds and grow to be three or more feet tall. They all have strong toes which they use to grab branches. They also have a long, colorful tail of feathers. These birds travel in big groups called flocks.

Both male and female macaws look alike, which is uncommon among vividly colored birds. They mate for life, and females lay the eggs while the males hunt for food. They speak to each other by making loud squawks or calls, and they sleep in flocks in the trees. Macaws can be seen in zoos around the world. They can also be found for sale in pet stores. Some species are endangered as they are fading away. Soon, they might be gone from the wild. It is important to protect this beautiful bird from extinction.

## a. Questions and Answers

1. In which forests are Macaws found?

______________________________________________

2. How long do Macaws live?

______________________________________________

3. How do these birds help in growing new tress in the forests?

______________________________________________

4. What are the responsibilities of the male and female macaws?

______________________________________________

5. How do the macaws communicate with each other?

______________________________________________

## b. Write one word for each of the phrases.

1. birds fading away ____________
2. gone from wild ____________
3. imitate the words ____________
4. make a loud harsh noise ____________
5. special ability at something ____________

**c. The statements below are incorrect. Read carefully and rewrite the correct statements.**

1. The macaw bird is part of the finch family.

   ---------------------------------------------

2. A macaw can mimic wild animals.

   ---------------------------------------------

3. They eat flesh of dead animals found in the forests.

   ---------------------------------------------

4. Macaws are huge birds and go up to eighty inches.

   ---------------------------------------------

5. Macaws travel in a group of 3-4 birds.

   ---------------------------------------------

**d. Make new words by adding or subtracting letters.**

1. eighty—y + een = ------------------------------
2. rainforest—orest + all =------------------------------
3. zoos—os + ne = ------------------------------
4. squawks—wks + d = ------------------------------
5. branch—ch+d = ------------------------------

# 7 MILKY WAY

What do you think of when you hear the words, "Milky Way"? Do you think of a candy bar? Well, there is another Milky Way, and you live in it. It is our galaxy!

A galaxy is a huge collection of gas, dust, and billions of stars and their solar systems. Scientists have learned that there are many galaxies in the outer space. The Milky Way is a spiral-shaped galaxy with swirls of stars spinning out from its center. It is called a spiral galaxy because when you view it from the top or bottom, it looks like a spinning pinwheel. Scientists believe there are about 200 billion stars in the Milky Way. One of these stars is the Sun.

There are eight planets in our galaxy that orbit the Sun. One of them is Earth. It is the third planet from the Sun. At the center of the Milky Way, there is one of the strangest and deadliest things in the universe: a black hole. Black holes are born when a giant star runs out of energy. Its gravity, or attractive force, is so strong that it pulls in anything that gets too close, including stars. So, we're lucky that Earth is located far away from the center! The Andromeda galaxy is the closest galaxy to the Milky Way and is about two million light-years away.

## a. Answer the questions.

1. What is Milky Way?

2. How do you define a galaxy?

3. How many stars are believed to be the part of Milky Way?

4. Why is black hole regarded strange and deadly?

5. What is Andromeda galaxy and how far is it from Milky Way?

## b. Make a list of verbs, nouns and adjectives in the passage.

| Verbs | Nouns | Adjectives |
| --- | --- | --- |
| | | |
| | | |
| | | |
| | | |
| | | |

## c. Rewrite each sentence with appropriate punctuation marks and capitalization.

1. a galaxy is a huge collection of gas dust and billions of stars and their solar system

   ----------------------------------------------------------------

2. black holes are born when a giant star runs out of energy

   ----------------------------------------------------------------

3. the andromeda galaxy is the closest galaxy to the milky way

   ----------------------------------------------------------------

4. earth is the third planet from the Sun

   ----------------------------------------------------------------

5. so we're lucky that earth is located far away from the center

   ----------------------------------------------------------------

## d. Choose the word that is most suitable.

| | a) | b) | c) |
|---|---|---|---|
| 1. collection | a) a group of things | b) put together | c) book |
| 2. spinning | a) dry | b) rapid turns | c) spit |
| 3. deadly | a) beautiful | b) dreamy | c) fatal |

# THE BACKYARD

8

Mosey and Jim are best friends. They are neighbors and spend a lot of time together. They also go to the same school. Although Mosey is a year younger to Jim but they really share a good bond. One misty morning, Mosey and Jim were looking around their backyard. They were sitting on the grass. Jim saw a rock with little plants on it.

"Look at that mossy green rock!" Jim cried. "That is not a rock," Mosey said. "It's a dinner table for snails." A snail inched over to the rock to munch on the plants. Next, Jim saw a leaf. "Look at that pretty yellow leaf!" Jim cried. "That is not a leaf," Mosey said. "It's a blanket for beetles." A beetle crawled under the warm leaf. Then, Jim saw a flower. "Look at that red flower!" Jim cried. "That is not a flower," Mosey said. "It's a shower for worms." A worm played in the water under the flower as dewdrops dripped from the petals. "Look at that wild mushroom!" Jim cried. "That is not a mushroom," Mosey said. "It's an umbrella for spiders." A spider knit a web under the mushroom away from the mist.

Finally, Jim saw a stick. "Look at that squiggly..." Jim stopped. If he called it a stick, Mosey would say it was not a stick. So, Jim cried, "Look at that squiggly ladybug ladder!" Mosey grinned at Jim and said, "Now you're seeing things from another point of view!" Mosey and Jim really like to spend their time sitting in their backyard and discussing about the marvels of the nature.

a. **Answer the questions.**

1. Where were Mosey and Jim in the morning?

   _______________________________________________

2. What did Jim see first?

   _______________________________________________

3. What did Mosey mean by "an umbrella for spiders"?

   _______________________________________________

4. How many creatures do Mosey and Jim spot in their backyard?

   _______________________________________________

5. What do you think the story is about?

   _______________________________________________

b. **Find the words in the passage which mean the same as the given phrases.**

1. twisty or curvy _______________
2. an object that helps you stay dry in the rain _______________
3. a tool you use to climb up and down _______________
4. water drops that form on plants and grass _______________
5. chomp or chew _______________

c. Do you have a special place in your house that you like the most? Write a few sentences about it?

_______________________________________________

_______________________________________________

_______________________________________________

_______________________________________________

_______________________________________________

_______________________________________________

_______________________________________________

d. Jim points out the following objects in the story. Match each object on the left to Mosey's description of it on the right.

| | |
|---|---|
| wild mushroom • | • dinner table for snails |
| mossy green rock • | • blanket for beetles |
| red flower • | • umbrella for spiders |
| yellow leaf • | • shower for worms |

# 9 HUMMINGBIRDS

A hummingbird is a small bird with a long, slender bill. Many hummingbirds have brightly colored, glittery feathers. Often the males are more colorful than the females. The most beautiful hummingbirds are found in the West Indies and South America. There are over 350 known hummingbird species, with new species being described every year.

The crest of the tiny head of these birds shines like a sparkling crown of colored light. The shades of color that adorn its breast are equally brilliant. As the bird flits from one flower to another, it looks more like a bright flash of sunlight than it does like a living being. Hummingbirds come in all sorts of shapes and sizes, but none of them are heavy. An average hummingbird might weigh around 4gm.

Why are they called hummingbirds? It is because they make a soft humming noise by the rapid motion of their wing—a motion so rapid—that as they fly, you can hardly see their wings.

The nest of the hummingbirds is about half the size of a very small hen's egg attached to a twig, no thicker than a steel knitting needle. It is made of cotton fibers and is covered with the softest bits of leaf and bark. The mother bird will dart if one approaches the spot where one of these birds has built its nest and it will try to peck you. Its sharp beak may hurt you. The poor little thing knows no other way of defending its young and instinct teaches it that you might carry off its nest if you find it.

**a. Answer the questions.**

1. Where are hummingbirds mainly found?

   ---

2. How do hummingbirds look?

   ---

3. How did the hummingbirds get their name?

   ---

4. What is the nest of a hummingbird made up of?

   ---

5. What might happen if you try to go close to the bird's nest?

   ---

**b. Identify the correctly spelled word.**

1. motion mosion motiun
2. fibare fibre fybar
3. instink instick instinct
4. flayh flash flaish
5. crest cresht kcrest

C. **Read each sentence and work out the meaning of the words in bold. Color the circle next to the correct answer.**

1. As the bird **flits** from one flower to another, it looks more like a bright flash of sunlight.

   ◯ move swiftly and lightly

   ◯ runs away

2. The head of hummingbirds **shines** like a sparkling crown of colored light.

   ◯ glow; reflects out bright light

   ◯ appears dull and dark

3. Hummingbirds make a soft, humming noise by the **rapid** motion of their wings.

   ◯ low value

   ◯ great speed; in short time

# OCTOPUSES

10

Octopuses are sea animals famous for their round bodies, bulging eyes and eight long arms. These cool critters live in all the world's oceans, but they're especially abundant in warm tropical waters. Octopuses are extremely intelligent. They have an oversized head which has a huge brain, making them a clever addition to the sea.

Octopuses don't have teeth or sharp claws to defend themselves. Octopuses like to hide themselves in the sand on the bottom of the ocean floor. It can change the color of its skin to match the sand. This color change, or camouflage, happens in less than a minute.

Some octopuses like to stay in shallow water because octopuses are invertebrates, meaning they don't have backbones, and can squeeze themselves into small spaces. Another way an octopus can hide is by shooting ink. An octopus uses a part of its body called a siphon to shoot ink into the water. The ink forms a cloud that hides the octopus. By the time the ink clears and the predator can see again, the octopus has swum away or hidden itself.

If an octopus loses one of its arms, it will grow back. There is one kind of octopus that has venom to use in defense. The blue-ringed octopus is tiny; it could fit in the palm of your hand. The blue-ringed octopus is very poisonous and can kill predators much larger than itself, including humans.

a. **Answer the following questions.**

1. What size is a blue-ringed octopus?

---------------------------------------------

2. What happens when an octopus shoots ink in water?

---------------------------------------------

3. Why do some octopuses like to stay in shallow water?

---------------------------------------------

4. How long does it take an octopus to camouflage?

---------------------------------------------

5. How do octopuses look?

---------------------------------------------

b. **Find the words in the passage which mean the same as the given phrases.**

1. disguise in a way of blending with the surroundings ------------
2. animal that hunts other animals ------------
3. to resist an attack ------------
4. with no backbone ------------

c. How does an octopus defend itself?

Ways an octopus defends itself

d. Unscramble the letters to form meaningful words.

1. i t e n l e g l i t n ____________

2. g c u f o a l a e m ____________

3. t r e p d a o r ____________

4. n e f d e s e ____________

5. z s e u q e e ____________

# 11 THE SMITHS

The Smiths have been living in Wellsboro for a very long time. Their whole family lives there. But Sam wants to relocate to a quite and less populated place.

So, one day Sam decided to move southwest along with his family. Sixteen-year-old Matt was happy. "I'm glad we are going," he said. "I feel crowded here. There are too many houses and too many people." Father prepared for the journey. He took out the big wagon and hitched two horses to it. Mother packed clothes, quilts, dishes, pots, pans and kettles. She would make food for the family along the way.

Matt tied a cow behind the wagon. The family said goodbye to the neighbors and to their old home and started on their way.

The Smiths traveled across Pennsylvania. On and on they went towards the new country. At last, the family came to the rolling green Yadkin Valley in North Carolina. There were a few houses there already, but it was much wider than in Pennsylvania.

Father said, "This is going to be a good farming land. We will stop here." Matt looked all about him. There was level land close by. There were woods not far away. There were mountains in the west.

Matt knew the hunting would be good. Father and the boy cut down trees and started to build a log house. Soon, the Smiths had a new home in the new land.

**a. Answer the questions that follow.**

1. Are Sam and Matt related? How?

 ______________________________________

2. How did the Smiths build a new home?

 ______________________________________

3. Where did the family finally stop?

 ______________________________________

4. How was the new place?

 ______________________________________

5. What did the father say regarding the new land they had come to?

 ______________________________________

**b. Arrange the sentences in correct order.**

The Smiths had a new home in the new land. ◯

Father prepared for the journey. ◯

Father and the boy cut down trees. ◯

The Smiths traveled across Pennsylvania. ◯

At last, the family came to the rolling green Yadkin Valley. ◯

**c. Find the words in the passage that are the opposite of words in bold. Rewrite the correct sentences.**

1. The family said good bye to the neighbors and to their **new** home.

_______________________________________________

2. Matt knew the hunting would be **bad**.

_______________________________________________

3. Matt tied a cow **In front** of the wagon.

_______________________________________________

4. Sixteen-year-old Matt was **unhappy**.

_______________________________________________

5. There was level land **far away** and there were woods **close by.**

_______________________________________________

# POLAR BEARS

12

Polar bears live along shores and on sea ice in the icy cold Arctic. When sea ice forms over the ocean in cold weather, many polar bears head to hunt. Considered talented swimmers, polar bears can sustain a speed of six miles per hour by paddling with their front paws and holding their hind legs flat like a rudder. They have a thick layer of body fat and a water-repellent coat that protects them from the cold air and water.

Polar bears spend over fifty per cent of their time hunting for food. Polar bears primarily eat seals. Polar bears often rest silently at a seal's breathing hole in the ice, waiting for a seal in the water to come to surface. A polar bear may also hunt by swimming beneath the ice. A polar bear might catch only one or two out of ten seals it hunts, depending on the time of year and other variables. Their diet mainly consists of ringed and bearded seals because they need large amounts of fat to survive. But climate change is making it harder for polar bears to hunt. Ice melts earlier and re-forms later than it has in the past. Without the sea ice, the polar bear must scavenge for other, less nutritious food. Polar bears are increasingly spending longer periods on land, where they are often attracted to areas where humans live.

a. **Answer the questions.**

1. Where do the polar bears live?

2. When do the polar bears hunt?

3. How do the polar bears keep themselves protected from cold air?

4. What will happen if there is no sea ice?

5. What does their diet mainly consist of?

b. **Make sentences with the given words.**

1. scavenge

2. survive

3. swim

4. hunt

**c. Choose the correct answer.**

1. Polar bears are

   a) good fighters

   b) great swimmers

   c) nocturnal animals

2. A polar bear spends

   a) half of their lifetime hunting for food

   b) a lifetime sleeping

   c) considerable time stealing food

3. Polar bears need

   a) large amounts of fat to survive

   b) less nutritious food

   c) spending longer periods on land

**d. Find the words in the passage which mean the same as the given words.**

1. keep up ______________________

2. essentially ______________________

3. capricious ______________________

4. rummage ______________________

5. skillful ______________________

# 13 READING IS A GOOD HABIT

Alex reads more than anyone he knows. He loves to read during his free time. His friends tease him because he would rather read than play video games, but his parents and his teachers are proud of him. They say reading is important, and it will help him learn about the world around him.

One day Alex and his class was assigned a science project about volcanoes. The assignment was to create a poster board with information about volcanoes and to build a volcano model. Alex ended up being in a group with Liz, Andy and Josh.

They went to the library to look for more information about volcanoes. Then they decided on the topic together. What causes volcanoes to erupt? The release of pressure when magma rises up through cracks in the Earth's crust causes volcanoes to erupt. How do volcanoes form? Lava from eruptions cools and forms new crust. The crust builds up after several eruptions to form a volcano. How hot is lava? Lava can get as hot as 1,165°F.

The next night they met at Josh's house to build their model of volcano. The volcano looked great. Alex, Liz, Andy and Josh were very proud of their hard work. When they turned in their project, their teacher was proud too. Thanks to Alex's good habit, they earned an A+ on both parts of the project.

## a. It's time for Q&A!

1. What is the one thing that Alex loves to do?

   ____________________________________________

2. Why does his friends tease him?

   ____________________________________________

3. What does Alex's parents and teachers say?

   ____________________________________________

4. What was the topic of the science project assigned to Alex and his class?

   ____________________________________________

5. Who all were in Alex's group of science project?

   ____________________________________________

## b. Complete the paragraph about volcanoes.

The release of pressure when magma ____________________ ____________________ to erupt. Lava ____________________ ____________________ new crust. The crust builds ____________________ volcano. Lava ____________________ °F.

c. **Write whether the statements are True or False.**

1. Alex and his friends went to the museum to look for more information about volcanoes. ___________

2. Alex's parents and his teachers are proud of him. ___________

3. The assignment was to create a poster board with information about animals. ___________

4. Magma rises up through cracks in the Earth's crust causing volcanoes to erupt. ___________

5. Alex ended up being in a group with Liz, Andy and Marc. ___________

d. **Let's make sentences!**

1. earn ______________________________________

2. assign ______________________________________

3. follow ______________________________________

4. proud ______________________________________

5. erupt ______________________________________

# COLORS

14

Artists use color to create patterns. Color can also show different moods. Bright colors make us feel happy and energetic. Dark colors make us feel calm or sad. To see color, you need to have light. When light shines on an object, some colors bounce off the object and others are absorbed by it. Our eyes only see the colors that are bounced off or reflected. The primary colors are red, yellow and blue. They are the colors that can be mixed together to make different colors. Mixing two primary colors makes a secondary color. The secondary colors are orange, green, and violet. Orange is made by mixing yellow and red. Green is made by mixing yellow and blue. Violet is made by mixing red and blue.

Intermediate colors can be made by mixing a primary and a secondary color together. Some intermediate colors are blue-violet and red-orange. Black, white, and gray are special colors. They are called neutral colors.

Colors have been organized into a color wheel. The color wheel was developed by Sir Isaac Newton by taking the color spectrum and bending it into a circle. The color wheel is the basis of color theory, because it shows the relationship between colors. It shows the three primary colors, three secondary colors and six intermediate colors. Artists use the color wheel. It helps them know which colors they want to use together. The color wheel can also be divided into warm and cool colors. Warm colors are the colors from red through to yellow. Cool colors are the colors from blue to green and purple.

**a. Answer the questions.**

1. How do artists create patterns?

---

2. What do bright colors make one feel?

---

3. Which are the three primary colors?

---

4. What are secondary colors?

---

4. What are blue-violet and red-orange colors called?

---

**b. Write the words which mean the same as given words.**

1. major ________________
2. combine ________________
3. in-between ________________
4. arranged ________________
5. lively ________________

**c. Fill in the blanks.**

1. Mixing two primary colors makes a ____________ color.

2. Colors have been organized into a color ____________.

3. ____________ colors can be made by mixing a ____________ and a secondary color together.

4. Violet is made by mixing ____________ and ____________.

5. There are ____________ intermediate colors.

**d. Complete the infographic.**

1. Select the primary colors.

2. What secondary color we get when we mix these primary colors? Tick the correct option.

# 15 FOOD IS FUEL

Everything that is alive needs energy. All animals get the energy they need from food. Think about the human body as an amazing machine. It can do all kinds of things for us. Food is the fuel that helps keep this amazing machine running.

Plants use sunlight to make their own food. Animals are not able to do that. Some animals eat plants and are known as herbivores while some eat other animals as meat and are called carnivores. Some animals, like humans eat both plants and animals. They are called omnivores.

Since plants make their own food using sunlight, the Sun's energy is found in plants. The Sun's energy is very strong. It loses a lot of its strength by the time it goes into a plant.

When we eat plants, we get more of the Sun's energy than when we eat animals. That's why it is good to eat fruits and vegetables. When an animal eats a plant, the energy is less strong as the animal also uses its energy to find the plant to eat. When a second animal eats the first animal, it gets even lesser energy than the first animal. The second animal uses a lot of energy to chase its prey.

Like a car that has to be filled with fuel, living things have to eat again and again. Instead of fuel, living things use food as fuel.

a. It's time for Q&A!

1. From where do the animals get energy?

---

2. What keeps the human body running like a machine?

---

3. What helps the plants make their own food?

---

4. Why is it good to eat fruits and vegetables?

---

5. What happens when a second animal eats the first animal?

---

b. What's the energy level?

| | High | Moderate | Low |
|---|---|---|---|
| 1. Plants make their food | | ____ | ____ |
| 2. Humans eat plants | | ____ | ____ |
| 3. First animal eat plants | | ____ | ____ |
| 4. Second animal eat plants | | ____ | ____ |

**c. Underline the incorrect word and rewrite the correct statements.**

1. Plants use rain to make their own food.

_______________________________________________

2. A car needs to be filled with water to keep it running.

_______________________________________________

3. When a second animal eats the first animal, it gets higher energy than the first animal.

_______________________________________________

4. It is bad to eat fruits and vegetables as it is a small source of energy.

_______________________________________________

**d. Define the following.**

1. Herbivore _______________________________________________

_______________________________________________

2. Carnivore _______________________________________________

_______________________________________________

3. Omnivore _______________________________________________

_______________________________________________

# NATURAL RESOURCES



Resources are things that we use. Natural resources come from Earth and many of our natural resources are limited. Air, water, trees, wood, soil, minerals, petroleum, metals, and sunlight are all examples. Some resources are renewable and can be replaced or grown. You can plant a new tree when you cut one down. Other resources are non-renewable. This means that they cannot be replaced or grown. You can dig coal out of the ground. Once the coal is used, it is gone.

Many of Earth's natural resources are limited, but people can help conserve those resources. When you try to conserve a natural resource, you use it less so that it does not get used up fast.

One way that people conserve fuel, like gasoline is by riding a bicycle or walking. This works well when the distance is short. We don't have to drive everywhere. Water is a very important natural resource. We all need it to live. We can conserve water by making sure that our pipes and faucets do not leak. We can also conserve water by making smart choices. One choice is to use the dishwasher and washing machine only when they are full. Another choice is to turn off the water when you brush your teeth. We can all make a difference!

Resources must be carefully managed to avoid misuse. Deforestation, mining and land development have transformed natural areas, destroying ecosystems and harming soil and water supplies.

## a. It's time for Q&A!

1. What is a renewable resource?

_______________________________________________

2. What does it mean to conserve resources?

_______________________________________________

3. How can we conserve fuel?

_______________________________________________

4. Why should we conserve water?

_______________________________________________

5. How are ecosystems destroyed?

_______________________________________________

## b. Make 5 words from the word RESOURCE

1. ________________________
2. ________________________
3. ________________________
4. ________________________
5. ________________________

**c. Choose the correct meaning of each word.**

1. conserve

   a) preserve b) destroy c) spend

2. important

   a) insignificant b) prime c) futile

3. limited

   a) ample b) finite c) plenty

**d. Based on your understanding, list a few renewable and non-renewable natural resources. Also mention your thoughts on how we can conserve resources.**

## 17 THE TALLEST TREES

Redwood trees are the tallest trees in the world. Some grow over 300 feet high, which is taller than a thirty-storey building. Redwoods get their common name from their bark and heartwood, the reddish-brown color which stems from high tannin levels. Think of it this way: If a six-feet tall man stood at the base of a redwood tree, the tree would be fifty times taller than the man!

These giant trees grow near the coast of California and Oregon. The climate is foggy and rainy there, which gives the redwoods a constant supply of water. Redwoods can grow for hundreds of years; in fact, some have lived for over 2,000 years! The bark is very thick, protecting the trees from insects, diseases and fires. Their thick bark holds large quantities of water, which protects them from periodic, naturally occurring fires. Redwood leaves are green, flat, and sharp-pointed. The brown cones are egg-shaped and two inches in diameter.

Redwood trees are very important to the lumber companies because the trees are so large that each one can be cut into lots of lumber. You may have seen lumber like this in redwood fences or redwood patio furniture. However, many of the trees are protected by law in the Redwood National Park. Lumber companies cannot cut trees that grow there. This is done so that the trees do not become extinct.

a. **Answer the given questions.**

1. How tall are redwood trees?

 ---------------------------------------

2. How did the redwood trees get their name?

 ---------------------------------------

3. Where do these trees grow?

 ---------------------------------------

4. How is the bark of redwood trees?

 ---------------------------------------

5. Why are redwood trees important to lumber companies?

 ---------------------------------------

b. **Find the words in the passage which mean the same as given phrases.**

1. no longer in existence ---------------
2. outer covering of trees ---------------
3. wood cut into boards ---------------
4. happens regularly ---------------
5. land by the sea ---------------

**c. Write whether the statements are True or False.**

1. Lumber companies can cut trees that grow in Redwood National Park. ___________
2. Redwoods can grow for hundreds of years. ___________
3. The bark of redwood trees is green in color. ___________
4. Redwood trees are the tallest trees in the world. ___________
5. Redwood trees grow near the coast of California and Oregon. ___________

**d. Choose the correct verb from the given box. Add 's' wherever necessary.**

| grow | live | cut | give | used | supply |
|---|---|---|---|---|---|

1. Redwoods can ___________ for hundreds of years.
2. Lumber companies cannot ___________ trees that grow in the Redwood National Park.
3. The foggy and rainy climate ___________ the redwoods a constant ___________ of water.
4. Redwood trees ___________ for over 2,000 years!
5. Lumber from redwoods is ___________ for fences or redwood patio furniture.

# SNAKES

18

Snakes are elongated, legless, carnivorous reptiles that can be distinguished from legless lizards by their lack of eyelids and external ears. Snakes are very good at hiding. Most snakes can camouflage themselves into their environment. That means they have different colors and patterns on their bodies that allow them to blend in with the colors and patterns of things around them.

Camouflage helps them hide from their enemies and helps them be sneaky when they are trying to catch something to eat. For example, the emerald tree boa lives in the jungle. Its green skin makes it nearly invisible among the green leaves of the trees.

Rattlesnakes live in rocky, dry places. The patterns of black, tan, and brown on their backs help them blend in with their rocky environment. The horned viper lives in the desert. Its skin is the same color as sand where it burrows underground. It is hard to see unless it is moving.

Also, some snakes that are harmless look very similar to venomous snakes. The harmless milk snake is colored orange, with yellow and black stripes, much like the poisonous coral snake. The enemies of the milk snake mistake it for a coral snake because they look so much alike.

Most species are non-venomous and those that have venom use it primarily to kill and subdue prey rather than for self-defense. Some possess venom potent enough to cause painful injury or even death to humans.

**a. Answer the following questions.**

1. How do the snakes blend in with the things around them?

---------------------------------------------

2. How does camouflage helps snakes?

---------------------------------------------

3. Why do snakes use their venom?

---------------------------------------------

4. Where does the horned viper live?

---------------------------------------------

**b. Write the antonyms and synonyms of the given words with the help of the word bank.**

safe merge harmful seize conceal
alike different free reveal

| WORDS | ANTONYMS | SYNONYMS |
|---|---|---|
| harmless | | |
| similar | | |
| capture | | |
| hide | | |

**c. Rearrange the jumbled words to make meaningful sentences.**

1. can / into / themselves / their / camouflage / snakes / environment

_____________________________________________

2. as / the / horned / skin / same / viper / color / sand / is

_____________________________________________

3. the / snake / for / a / milk / mistake / of / the / enemies / coral / snake / it

_____________________________________________

4. snakes / look / some / to / are / snakes / very / similar / harmless / venomous

_____________________________________________

**d. Explain how the below species of snake camouflages?**

| Snake | Where do they live? | How do they camouflage? |
|---|---|---|
| emerald tree boa | | |
| rattlesnake | | |
| horned viper snake | | |

# 19 EARTHQUAKES

Earthquakes are one of the most powerful events on the earth. When large sections of underground rock break and move suddenly, an earthquake occurs. This causes the ground to shake back and forth. Small earthquakes do not cause much damage, but large ones do. Some earthquakes have caused buildings and bridges to fall. Others have caused rivers to change their paths.

Earthquakes near mountains and cliffs can cause landslides that cover up the houses and roads below. If a massive earthquake occurs under the ocean, it can cause giant waves which flood the seashore. When high-intensity earthquakes occur in a city, there is danger of fire from broken gas lines and electric lines. Broken telephone lines and damaged roads make it difficult for rescue workers to help people who are in need.

Scientists are trying to find ways to predict an earthquake so that people can be warned ahead of time. Earthquakes are measured using observations from seismometers.

The ancient Chinese used a device that looked like a jar with dragons on the top surrounded by frogs with their mouths open. When an earthquake occurred, a ball fitted into each dragon's mouth would drop out of the dragon's mouth into the frog's. The position of the frog which received a ball indicated the direction of the earthquake. This was one of the first tools to help figure out where an earthquake originated from.

a. **Answer the given questions.**

1. How does an earthquake occur?

______________________________________________

2. What causes the most damage?

______________________________________________

3. What do the earthquakes near mountains do?

______________________________________________

4. What happens during a high-intensity earthquake in cities?

______________________________________________

5. What makes it difficult for the rescue workers?

______________________________________________

b. **Circle the adjectives and underline the nouns.**

1. A massive earthquake can cause giant waves.
2. Some big earthquakes have caused buildings and bridges to fall.
3. Earthquakes can cause giant waves which flood the seashore.
4. Earthquakes near mountains and cliffs can cause major landslides.
5. Broken telephone lines and damaged roads make the rescue difficult.

### c. Complete the sentences

1. If a massive earthquake ______________________________ cause ______________________________ seashore.

2. Broken ______________________________ make it difficult ______________________________ need.

3. Earthquakes near mountains ______________________________ and roads below.

### d. Let's make sentences!

1. danger ______________________________

2. broken ______________________________

3. predict ______________________________

4. damage ______________________________

5. giant ______________________________

# HOW TO MAKE ICE CREAM 20

Ice cream is a frozen dessert typically made from dairy products, such as milk and cream, and it is often combined with fruits or other ingredients and flavors. Can you make your own ice cream at home? Yes, you can make ice cream at home, but it's not as simple as baking a cake. While there are ice cream-making machines that make this process easier, it's not mandatory to have one. First, gather your materials. You will need milk, sugar, and vanilla essence as ingredients for the ice cream. You will also need some other materials like two zip-top plastic bags, ice, and salt. One of the zip-top plastic bags should be larger than the other. In the smaller bag, combine 1 cup of milk, about 2 tablespoons of sugar, and a teaspoon of vanilla essence. Close the zip tightly! Use your hands to squish the bag to mix the ingredients, or shake the bag. In the larger bag, combine between 2–4 cups of ice and about a cup of salt.

Put the smaller bag into the larger bag, making sure the small bag is still closed tightly. Close the larger bag. Shake the bags for at least 5 minutes. Take a peek at the smaller bag, if it looks like ice cream, pour the ice cream into a bowl, and enjoy your treat! If it still looks thin, shake the bag for a few more minutes before enjoying. When you feel successful at making plain vanilla ice cream, experiment with adding different ingredients to make your own delicious flavors.

In the US, July is named the national ice cream month. Before milk-based ice cream was introduced in the 10th century, this summer treat was made from actual ice. The recipe for ice cream arrived in North America about 250 years after Christopher Columbus discovered America.

## a. It's time for Q&A!

1. What are the ingredients for making an ice cream?

---

2. What are the other materials required?

---

3. What should be done if the ice cream still looks thin?

---

4. When is National Ice Cream month observed in the US?

---

5. What is ice cream typically made of?

---

## b. Which is your favorite ice cream and why?

---

---

---

---

c. Find the words in the passage which mean the same as the given words.

1. victorious _ _ _ _ _ _ _ _ _ _ _ _ _ _ _ _ _ _

2. trial _ _ _ _ _ _ _ _ _ _ _ _ _ _ _ _ _ _

3. jiggle _ _ _ _ _ _ _ _ _ _ _ _ _ _ _ _ _ _

4. peep _ _ _ _ _ _ _ _ _ _ _ _ _ _ _ _ _ _

5. decant _ _ _ _ _ _ _ _ _ _ _ _ _ _ _ _ _ _

d. Arrange the steps in the right order.

Close the zip tightly! ◯

If it looks like ice cream, pour the ice cream into a bowl, and enjoy your treat! ◯

In the larger bag, combine between 2–4 cups of ice and about a cup of salt. ◯

Squish the bag to mix the ingredients, or shake the bag. ◯

Put the smaller bag into the larger bag and shake the bags for at least 5 minutes. ◯

Combine 1 cup of milk, about 2 tablespoons of sugar, and a teaspoon of vanilla essence. ◯

# 21 ALICE IN WONDERLAND

It was a warm summer day and Alice was getting bored sitting beside her sister. Suddenly, a little white rabbit with pink eyes ran in front of her shouting, "Oh dear, I'm late," and then disappeared down a rabbit's hole. "I must find out why he's in such a hurry!" cried Alice. She ran to the rabbit's hole and peeped through the entrance. The hole widened suddenly and Alice fell. Finally, she landed in a narrow hallway with doors of many sizes. On a table, Alice found a tiny gold key and a green bottle that said "DRINK ME." She drank it. Alice began to shrink until she was no bigger than a doll. She opened the door and quickly ran through it. "What a splendid garden!" she exclaimed. But the excitement soon wore off.

"I want to be big again," she shouted. Alice went looking for help. Soon, she saw a green caterpillar. He was sitting on the top of a large mushroom. "One side makes you big, the other side makes you small," he answered. Alice ate a piece of the mushroom. "Thank goodness, I'm growing!" Alice continued her walk. In the middle of a field, the Queen of Hearts was playing croquet. "Have you ever played croquet?" the Queen asked Alice. "Yes," Alice answered. "Play with me!" ordered the Queen. "And let me win or I'll have your head!" Alice won the game and the Queen ordered, "Off with her head!" Alice felt someone touch her shoulder, "Wake up. You've been sleeping for too long," said her sister softly. "I had a strange dream," said Alice.

**a. Answer the given questions.**

1. What did Alice see when she was sitting with her sister?

-------------------------------------------------

2. What happened when Alice peeped through the hole?

-------------------------------------------------

3. How did Alice shrink to the size of a doll?

-------------------------------------------------

4. Who helped Alice to grow back into her size?

-------------------------------------------------

5. Whom did Alice see in the middle of a field?

-------------------------------------------------

**b. Write the three forms of verbs.**

| | | | |
|---|---|---|---|
| go | | | |
| play | | | |
| sleep | | | |
| dream | | | |
| bore | | | |

c. **Who said these lines?**

1. "Oh dear, I'm late." ___________
2. "One side makes you big, the other side makes you small." ___________
3. "Wake up. You've been sleeping for too long." ___________
4. "I must find out why he's in such a hurry!" ___________
5. "Have you ever played croquet?" ___________

d. **Replace the nouns in bold with pronouns.**

1. ___________ **Alice** ran to the rabbit's hole and peeped through the entrance.
2. ___________ Alice saw a caterpillar. **The caterpillar** was sitting on the top of a large mushroom.
3. ___________ Alice was getting bored sitting beside **Alice's** sister.
4. ___________ The hole widened suddenly and **Alice** fell.
5. ___________ Alice felt someone touch **Alice's** shoulder.

# THE SHOEMAKER

22

A shoemaker and his wife lived in a little house on the edge of the woods. They were very poor, and they had nothing left in the house except for leather for one pair of shoes.

“I will cut out this last pair of shoes,” the shoemaker said to his wife. “Tomorrow I will sew them and peg them.” So, he cut out the leather and left it on his bench. The next morning, he went into his shop to make the shoes. What did he see? A pair of shoes all nicely made and ready to be sold. With the money, the poor shoemaker bought leather for two pairs of shoes. So, he cut out the leather for the shoes and left it on his bench.

The next morning when he went into his shop to make the shoes, what did he find? Yes, there were two pairs of shoes already made.

With the money, the poor shoemaker bought enough leather for four pairs of shoes. Again, he cut out the leather and left it on his bench. The next morning, he found four pairs of beautiful shoes, all well made. And so, it went on and on. Instead of being a very poor shoemaker, he became a very rich shoemaker. His shoes were so well made that even the Queen bought and wore them.

One day the couple decided to see who helps them. So, the next night they hid behind a curtain and saw some elves sewing the shoes. Seeing this, the wife also sewed the elves two pair of clothes and left them with the leather as a token of thank you. The elves were delighted to see the clothes and started dancing with excitement.

a. **Answer the questions.**

1. Where did the shoemaker live?

------------------------------------------------

2. What did the shoemaker do with the money he earned by selling shoe

------------------------------------------------

3. Which material were the shoes mostly made of?

------------------------------------------------

4. How did the shoemaker get rich?

------------------------------------------------

5. Who bought shoes from the shoemaker?

------------------------------------------------

b. **Why do you think the elves helped the shoemaker to make the shoes? Use your imagination and write a few sentences.**

------------------------------------------------

------------------------------------------------

------------------------------------------------

------------------------------------------------

------------------------------------------------

**c. State whether the statements are True or False.**

1. The shoemaker and his wife lived in a palace. __________

2. The shoemaker got very poor after selling the shoes. __________

3. The Queen bought the shoes from the shoemaker. __________

4. Every morning the shoemaker used to find ready-to-sell shoes on the bench. __________

5. The quality of shoes make by the shoemaker was very bad. __________

**d. Insert punctuation to fix the sentences.**

| comma (,) |
| --- |
| full stop (.) |
| question mark (?) |

1. So he cut out the leather and left it on his bench

2. Yes there were two pairs of shoes already made

3. Shoemaker went into his shop to make the shoes what did he find

4. He went into his shop to make the shoes What did he see

# 23 MARIE CURIE

Marie Curie was one of the most accomplished scientists in history. Together with her husband, Pierre, she discovered Radium, an element widely used for treating cancer, and studied Uranium and other radioactive substances. Pierre and Marie's amicable collaboration later helped to unlock the secrets of the atom.

Marie and Pierre Curie were married in 1895 and spent many productive years working together in the Physics laboratory. A short time after they discovered Radium, Pierre was killed by a horse-drawn wagon in 1906. Marie was stunned by this horrible misfortune and endured heartbreaking anguish. The fact that she had two young daughters to raise by herself greatly increased her distress.

Curie's feeling of despair finally began to fade when she was asked to succeed her husband as a Physics professor at the Sorbonne. She was the first woman to be given a professorship at the world-famous university. In 1911, she received the Nobel Prize in chemistry for isolating Radium.

Although Marie Curie eventually suffered a fatal illness from her long exposure to Radium, she never became disillusioned about her work. Regardless of the consequences, she dedicated herself to Science and to revealing the mysteries of the physical world.

a. Answer the given questions.

1. Who was Pierre Curie?

_______________________________________________

2. What is Marie's contribution towards science?

_______________________________________________

3. How did Marie's husband die?

_______________________________________________

4. What increased Marie's distress?

_______________________________________________

5. Why was Marie called to Sorbonne?

_______________________________________________

b. Find the words in the passage that are opposite of the given words.

1. enthusiastic ________________

2. indifferent ________________

3. conceal ________________

4. precede ________________

5. harmless ________________

**c. Fill in the blanks with the correct form of the verb.**

1. Marie was the first woman to be _ _ _ _ _ _ _ _ _ (give) a professorship.

2. Marie Curie _ _ _ _ _ _ _ _ _ _ (suffer) a fatal illness from her long exposure to Radium.

3. Marie had _ _ _ _ _ _ _ _ _ _ (dedicate) herself to science.

4. Pierre Curie and Marie, together worked towards _ _ _ _ _ _ _ _ _ _ (unlock) the secrets of the atom.

5. Marie was _ _ _ _ _ _ _ _ _ _ (stun) by this horrible misfortune.

**d. Review each set of words. Circle the misspelled word and rewrite the correct spelling.**

| | | | |
|---|---|---|---|
| woman | radium | scynce | _ _ _ _ _ _ _ _ _ _ _ _ _ _ _ _ |
| first | fisycs | world | _ _ _ _ _ _ _ _ _ _ _ _ _ _ _ _ |
| receeved | long | fade | _ _ _ _ _ _ _ _ _ _ _ _ _ _ _ _ |
| secrit | unlock | atom | _ _ _ _ _ _ _ _ _ _ _ _ _ _ _ _ |
| suffer | eyesolate | history | _ _ _ _ _ _ _ _ _ _ _ _ _ _ _ _ |

# ROBERT BRUCE AND THE SPIDER 24

There was once a king of Scotland whose name was Robert Bruce. He was both brave and wise. The king of England was at war with him, and had led a great army into Scotland to drive him out of the land.

Robert Bruce fought battle after battle. Six times Bruce led his brave little army against his foes; and six times his men were beaten, and driven into flight. Robert Bruce then escaped into a jungle and hid himself inside a cave. He was very depressed. He was ready to lose all hopes. As he lay on the cold ground thinking about giving up, he saw a little spider.

The spider was trying to finish weaving its web on the caves roof, but somehow it kept slipping down. The spider rose inch by inch on the thread of its web but fell down when it was just a few inches away from its destination. The king noticed, every time the spider slipped, it climbed back more carefully than before. The spider repeated the attempts to climb many a time, but fell down. The spider did not lose his heart and finally succeeded in its tenth attempt.

Robert Bruce was astonished at the courage and determination of the spider, this filled the king with new hope and strength. He learnt an important lesson from this tiny creature. He came out of the hiding, gathered his forces and led a very strong attack on the British forces. He was able to defeat his enemy this time. The king won his kingdom back.

**a. Answer the questions.**

1. Who was Robert Bruce?

_____________________________________________

2. What did Robert Bruce try doing?

_____________________________________________

3. Where did Robert Bruce flee?

_____________________________________________

4. What was the spider trying?

_____________________________________________

5. What lesson did Robert Bruce learn from the spider?

_____________________________________________

**b. Complete the text with the conjunctions 'and', 'but' or 'so'.**

Robert Bruce escaped into a jungle ____________ hid himself inside a cave. He was very depressed. The spider was trying to finish weaving its web on the caves roof, _________ somehow it kept slipping down. The spider rose inch by inch on the thread of its web __________ fell down when it was just a few inches away from its destination.

The spider repeated the attempts to climb, many a time, __________ fell down. The spider did not lose his heart __________ finally the spider succeeded in its tenth attempt.

**c. Rearrange the jumbled letters to form meaningful words and then make sentences using them.**

1. c b o e w b ____________________________________

____________________________________________

2. t a t m e t p ____________________________________

____________________________________________

3. m c i b l ____________________________________

____________________________________________

4. t c p a r e u ____________________________________

____________________________________________

5. d e f e t a ____________________________________

____________________________________________

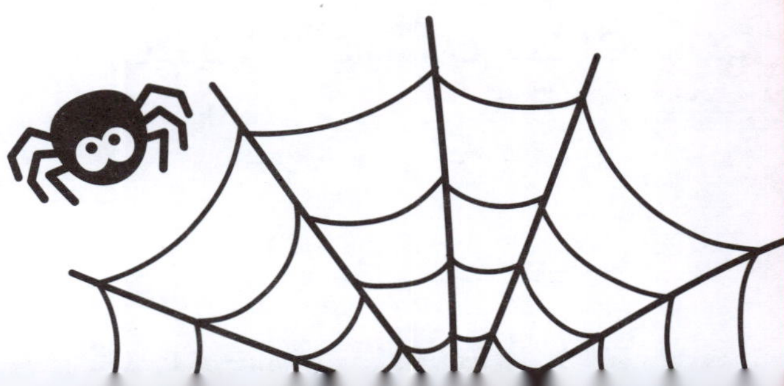

# 25 THE CAP SELLER AND THE MONKEYS

There was once a cap seller in a city. He used to go from village to village to sell caps. It was a hot summer day. The cap seller once was going to a fair to sell the caps. His way lay through a thick forest and he was tired, so he decided to take some rest under a big shady tree. Soon he was fast asleep.

There lived many monkeys on the tree. They saw him wearing a cap on his head. They came down, opened his bundle and took the caps and wore them on their heads. Then they climbed up on the high branches of the tree. After some time, the cap seller woke up. He found that his caps were missing. He felt very gloomy and looked around for them.

All of a sudden, he looked up and saw the monkeys wearing the caps. He tried very hard but could not get his caps back from the monkeys. The cap seller became very upset, he shouted at the monkeys in the tree. The monkeys yelled back at him. This made the cap seller more irritated. He picked up few stones from the ground and threw them at the monkeys. This time the monkeys threw the fruits they had in their hands at the cap seller. After his futile efforts he sat on the ground hopeless.

Suddenly, an idea struck his mind. He at once took off his own cap and threw it on the ground. He knew that monkeys are good imitators. Seeing him, the monkeys also threw their caps down. Now the cap seller was glad that his trick worked and he collected all his caps and went his way to the fair.

**a. It's time to answer the questions!**

1. Where was the cap seller headed?

---

2. Why did the cap seller sit under a big shady tree?

---

3. Who lived on the tree?

---

4. What did the monkeys do?

---

5. What did the cap seller do to get his caps back?

---

**b. Combine each sentence by adding comma and words in the bracket.**

1. He was so tired. He decided to take some rest under a big shady tree. (so)

---

2. Monkeys came down, opened his bundle. They took the caps and wore them on their heads. (and)

---

3. He tried very hard. He could not get his caps back from the monkeys. (but)

---

4. He knew that monkeys are good imitators. The monkeys also threw their caps down. (so)

---

**c. Find the plurals of the given words in the grid.**

| | | | | | | | | | | | |
|---|---|---|---|---|---|---|---|---|---|---|---|
| B | U | N | D | L | E | S | I | G | G | I | D |
| I | I | J | A | Y | P | D | U | C | L | I | N |
| T | T | D | H | T | R | E | E | S | E | O | O |
| E | O | R | S | H | E | L | L | P | B | W | I |
| S | L | I | I | B | I | A | R | S | N | Q | D |
| E | U | H | L | C | E | T | A | K | S | D | E |
| V | N | M | O | N | K | E | Y | S | S | Y | A |
| D | G | H | O | P | E | S | O | S | A | N | S |
| A | H | A | Z | K | U | M | L | Y | R | A | F |
| I | B | R | A | N | C | H | E | S | G | S | I |
| D | I | M | I | T | A | T | O | R | S | T | N |
| H | E | A | D | S | L | T | A | M | E | Y | C |

Bundle
Monkey
Branch
Idea
Tree
Trick
Head
Imitator
Hope

# BETTY'S BABY BIRD



Pip and Dad were making a new fence. Dad was doing the hammering and Pip was passing him the nails. Suddenly, Pip noticed Betty. "Dad," he cried. "Betty's got a baby bird in her hand." "Come here, Betty," called Dad. "Bring it here." Betty came towards Dad. She was carrying the bird very carefully. Betty dropped the bird in front of Dad. "Is it hurt?" asked Pip. "It seems all right," said Dad. "But it's frightened."

"What kind of bird is it?" asked Pip. "It's a baby thrush," said Dad. "Pick it up gently, Pip and we'll find a safe place for it." "How can we help it, Dad?" he asked. "We'll put it under a bush," said Dad, "If its parents are nearby, they'll come and feed it." Pip put the baby bird down in the shade, "What does a thrush eat?" he asked Dad. "Thrushes eat worms, snails and insects," said Dad. "If its parents don't come today, I'll call the Bird Rescue Centre," said Dad. "Let's bring the thrush inside, Dad," said Pip.

Pip put some dry grass in a box, when he put the baby bird in the box; it squeaked and opened its beak. "It must be very hungry," said Dad. He called the Bird Lady. She said, "Tonight you could feed it some hard-boiled egg." The thrush opened its beak wide and Pip dropped the food in. The next morning, Pip and Dad took the baby bird to the Bird Rescue Centre.

The Bird Lady showed them around. There were lots of baby birds. There were birds with broken wings and birds with broken legs. "Your baby bird will stay here until it can fly," the Bird Lady said.

## a. Who said this to whom?

| | Who said | To whom |
|---|---|---|
| 1. "Come here, Betty." | ___________ | ___________ |
| 2. "Tonight you could feed it some hard-boiled egg." | ___________ | ___________ |
| 3. "What kind of bird is it?" | ___________ | ___________ |
| 4. "We'll put it under a bush." | ___________ | ___________ |

## b. Tick the correct answer.

1. Whom did Dad call for help?

   (a) Pip ☐

   (b) Betty ☐

   (c) Bird Lady ☐

2. What does a thrush eat?

   (a) worms, snails and insects ☐

   (b) leaves, veggies and berries ☐

   (c) egg, bread and milk ☐

3. How did the bird react when Pip put it in the box?

   (a) squeaked and slept ☐

   (b) squeaked and opened its beak ☐

   (c) flew away ☐

c. **Write the names of the things that are related to the word Bird.**
**(Hints: example, sound, food, color, shape, size, place, etc.)**

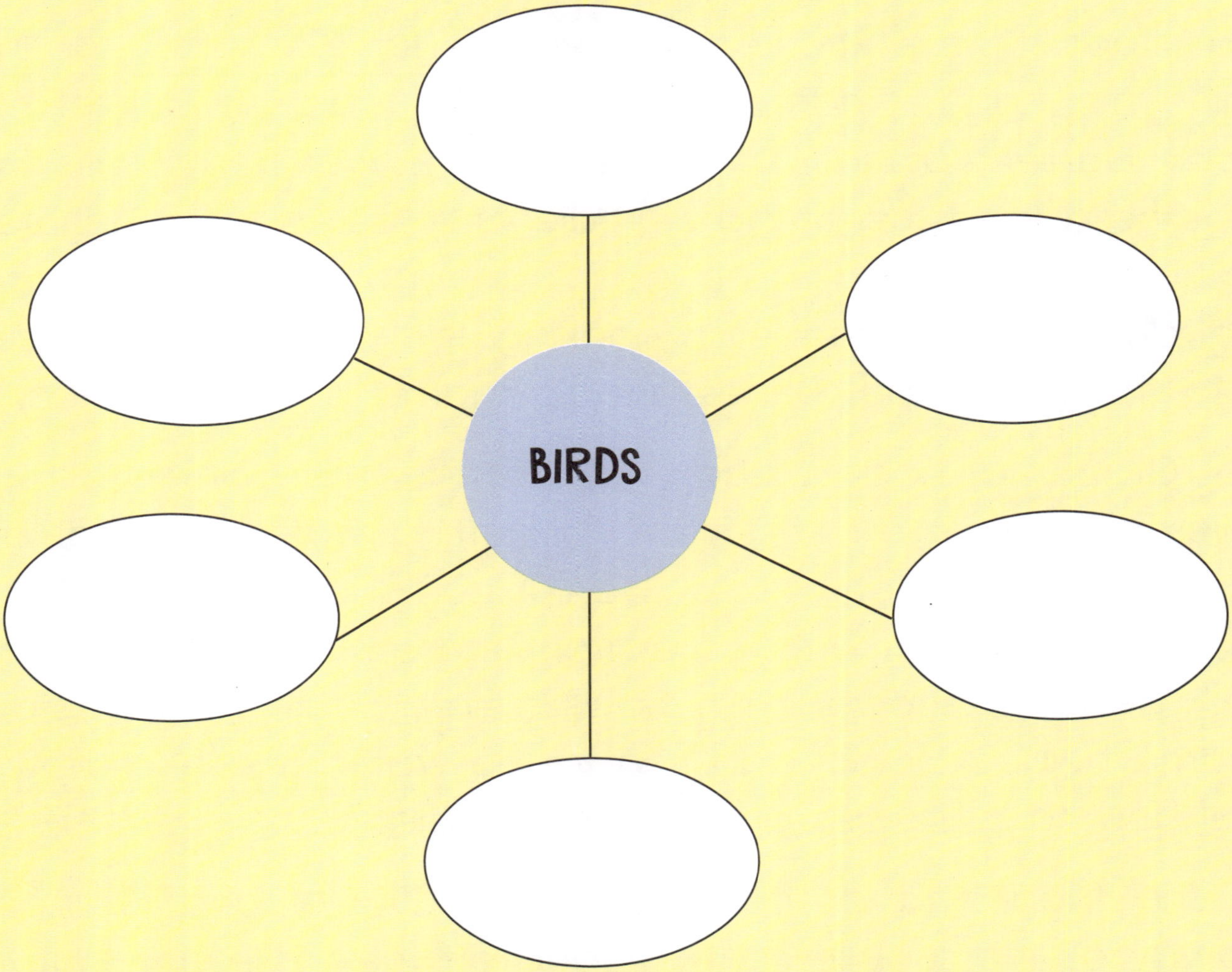


d. **Fill in the blanks with the appropriate words.**

1. The thrush opened its __________ wide and Pip dropped the __________ in.
2. Dad was doing the __________ and Pip was passing him the __________ .
3. Pip put some __________ in a box, when he put the baby bird in the box.
4. Thrushes eat __________ snails and __________ .

# 27 DANIEL AND HIS GRANDMA

Daniel stood in the kitchen. He waited for Grandma to finish washing her hands. Today, Grandma was teaching Daniel how to cook. Daniel was not just excited, but he was nervous as well! What if he added the wrong ingredients or put in too much salt? Then his food wouldn't taste good, and no one would eat it. Daniel always wanted to learn cooking. It is his passion. He really likes to make delicious dishes and Grandma is his inspiration.

Once Grandma had washed her hands, he pointed to the supplies on the table. "Let's start by putting water in a pot and letting it boil," Grandma said. Daniel could do that. He found the large pot, filled it with water from the sink, and put it on the stove. Grandma showed him how to safely turn on the stove. Grandma helped Daniel add rice to the water. She also showed Daniel how to grill slices of chicken in a flat pan.

Soon, the food had all been prepared. Daniel and Grandma put away all the supplies. They wiped off the table and put out plates, forks, and napkins. Then they sat at the table to eat. Would the food be good or bad? Daniel took the first bite. He chewed slowly. Then he smiled.

"Good?" asked Grandma. "Good," said Daniel, and he ate everything on his plate. Daniel now helps his Grandma cook everyday. When he grows up, he plans to open his own restaurant.

a. Let's answer the following questions.

1. Why was Daniel waiting for Grandma?

---

2. Why was Daniel nervous?

---

3. What did Grandma and Daniel do to start the cooking?

---

b. Make sentences with the past participle form of verbs.

1. chew ______________________________

______________________________

2. sit ______________________________

______________________________

3. teach ______________________________

______________________________

4. put ______________________________

______________________________

5. cook ______________________________

______________________________

**c. Write [T] for True and [F] for False statements in the box.**

1. Daniel and Grandpa prepared the food. ☐
2. They started by putting oil in a pot and letting it boil. ☐
3. Daniel ate everything on his plate. ☐
4. Grandma and Daniel sat at the table to eat. ☐
5. Grandma showed Daniel how to safely turn on the stove. ☐

**d. Write contracted form of the words in circle and expanded forms in the box.**

1. Daniel's food wouldn't taste good.

   Daniel's food [ ] taste good.

2. Let's start by putting water in a pot.

   [ ] start by putting water in a pot.

3. Daniel was not just excited, but he was nervous as well.

   Daniel ( ) just excited, but he was nervous as well.

4. Daniel's waiting for grandma.

   [ ] waiting for grandma.

5. They had put out plates, forks, and napkins.

   ( ) put out plates, forks, and napkins.

# GECKOS

28

Geckos are sometimes called lizards, and there are many species of them. They live all over the world and can survive in many climates. They have been found in deserts, mountains, rainforests, and even in snow.

Over a long period of time, geckos have developed special physical features to help them survive and avoid predators. Gecko tails serve many purposes. They help balance their weight as they climb branches,they act as fuel tanks to store fat, and as camouflage to help them disappear into their environment. Did you know that they can shed their tail? If the tail is grabbed or hurt, the gecko can shed it and it will grow back later. The tail makes up about half the length of the whole body. Some are as short as an inch, others are as long as fifteen inches. Most geckos are around six inches long.

Geckos are good climbers. Their feet have small, sticky pads that help them grip tree branches or rocks. Some types also have claws, which help them climb.

Most geckos are nocturnal, which means they sleep during the day and come out to play at night, but not all of them. Whenever they are awake, they like to eat bugs, insects, or fruit. As they store many nutrients in their tail, it's important that it grows back when it's shed.

Geckos can be of many different colors, from green to tan to pink. These small lizards can blend in by changing colors as needed and this is called camouflage. It has many abilities that help it survive, and it truly is an amazing creature.

**a. Answer each of the questions.**

1. Where are Geckos found?

_______________________________________________

2. What happens when a Gecko's tail is grabbed or hurt?

_______________________________________________

3. What kind of feet do Gecko's have?

_______________________________________________

4. What do Geckos eat?

_______________________________________________

5. What color are Geckos?

_______________________________________________

**b. Make as many words as you can with each of the given words.**

1. Rainforest _______________________________________________

_______________________________________________

2. Branch _______________________________________________

_______________________________________________

3. Important _______________________________________________

_______________________________________________

**c. Complete the crossword puzzle with the help of the given clues.**

Across

3. Geckos have great sticky pads making them great __________

4. It is stored in their tail __________

6. Geckos are sometimes called __________

Down

1. Changing color to blend with the surroundings __________

2. Geckos come out to play at this time __________

5. Geckos can shed this part of their body __________

# 29 KATHY, THE PRINCESS!

Kathy frowned as she watched the school bus drive away. Her brother Jake was leaving for school, but she could not go because she was sick. Today was a special day at school. They would be having a talent show, and she would miss it.

Someone knocked on her bedroom door. Mom came in. "How's my princess?" Mom asked. "I have something exciting planned for today." Mom smiled and pulled out a bag. Kathy opened the bag and gasped. Inside, she found a crown, a wand, and a princess book. "You are my princess for today," Mom said. "Put on your crown, and keep your wand close!" Kathy put on the shiny crown. She and Mom read the book about princesses. They pretended to do magic with the wand. They had a tea party. Soon, the school bus arrived again. Kathy's brother Jake was home. "Does this mean I'm not a princess anymore?" Kathy asked.

Mom smiled. "The day isn't over yet!" Mom and Jake did a funny performance for Kathy. She clapped and laughed. Then they ate snacks and watched a movie together. "I like being a princess," Kathy said with a sigh. Mom hugged Kathy. "Don't worry," she said. "You are always my princess."

Next day when Kathy went to her school, she told all her friends about how she spent her day at home as a princess and the fun she had with her mom and brother Jake.

a. **Answer the given questions.**

1. Why didn't Kathy go to school?

   ______________________________________________

2. What was so special about the day at school?

   ______________________________________________

3. Who came to cheer up Kathy?

   ______________________________________________

4. What was inside the bag?

   ______________________________________________

5. What had Mom planned for the day?

   ______________________________________________

b. **Write words from the passage that rhyme with the given set of words.**

1. wool, pool, cool ____________________
2. bore, door, floor ____________________
3. drown, brown, clown ____________________
4. fake, bake, cake ____________________
5. bond, fond, pond ____________________

c. **Fill in the blanks.**

1. Mom and Jake did a funny _________ for Kathy.

2. Kathy and Mom read the book about _________.

3. Kathy frowned as she watched the __________drive away.

4. Kathy, Mom and _________ate snacks and watched a movie togethe

5. Kathy had a __________at her school.

d. **If you were made a prince/princess for a day, how would you spend that day? Write a few sentences about it.**

______________________________________________

______________________________________________

______________________________________________

______________________________________________

______________________________________________

______________________________________________

______________________________________________

______________________________________________

# PATRICK, THE RABBIT 30

Once upon a time there were four little rabbits, and their names were Flipsy, Mipsy, Cottony and Patrick. They lived with their mother underneath the root of a very big fir tree.

"Now my dears," said Mrs Rabbit. "You may go into the fields, but don't go into Mr Gregg's garden. Now, run along, and don't get into mischief." Flipsy, Mipsy, and Cottony, who were good little bunnies, went down the lane to gather blackberries, but Patrick, who was naughty, ran into Mr Gregg's garden!

First, Patrick ate some lettuces and some French beans, but round the end of a cucumber frame, he came face to face with Mr Gregg! Mr Gregg was on his hands and knees planting young cabbages. As he saw Patrick, he jumped up and ran after him, and called out, "Stop." He lost his shoes among the cabbages and potatoes. Patrick sat down to rest; after a time, he began to wander about. He began to cry. Then he tried to find the gate! Patrick never stopped running or looked behind him till he got home to the big fir tree. Patrick was not very well during the evening. His mother put him to bed, and made some tea; and gave a dose of medicine to Patrick! "One tablespoonful to be taken at bedtime."

But Flipsy, Mipsy, and Cottony had bread and milk and blackberries for supper.

a. **Let's answer the following questions.**

1. How many siblings did Patrick have?

---

2. What did Patrick's mom tell them?

---

3. What did Patrick do after defying his mom?

---

4. Did Mr Gregg catch Patrick?

---

5. What happened to Patrick in the evening?

---

b. **Let's arrange the following words in alphabetical order.**

| four | mother | evening | naughty | lane |
|---|---|---|---|---|
| home | bed | tea | rest | wander |

---

---

---

c. Put the words given in the box into the following groups.

| field | potato | blackberry | cherry | beans |
|---|---|---|---|---|
| | tree | lettuce | sky | |

Fruits ______________________________________

Vegetables ______________________________________

Nature ______________________________________

d. Write the correct words.

| ONE | MANY |
|---|---|
| rabbit | __________ |
| __________ | cabbages |
| __________ | beans |
| potato | __________ |
| __________ | shoes |
| bunny | __________ |
| lettuce | __________ |
| __________ | blackberries |

# 31 THE SOLAR SYSTEM

The universe is massive. It is mostly empty space. Galaxies and clusters of galaxies that make up the visible universe are concentrated in a complex scaffold that surrounds enormous empty spaces. It is much bigger than we can imagine and our solar system is just a small part of it. Our solar system houses a big, bright star called the Sun. The Sun is a rich source of electromagnetic energy that it exudes in the form of heat and light. There are eight planets in our solar system namely, Mercury, Venus, Earth, Mars, Jupiter, Saturn, Uranus and Neptune. These planets revolve around the Sun in a fixed path referred to as the orbit. Several other smaller objects also move around the Sun.

Many planets in our solar system have natural satellites called the moon. While Earth has one moon, Mars has two, Neptune has 14 moons, Uranus has 27 moons, Saturn has 62 moons and Jupiter has as many as 79 moons. Even the dwarf planet Pluto has 5 moons. Mercury and Venus, on the other hand, do not have any moon. Just as the planets move around the Sun in a fixed path, moons orbit around their respective planets.

In addition to the Sun, planets and moons, our solar system consists of several other celestial bodies like comets, asteroids and meteoroids. While our solar system has only one star, many other solar systems are known to have at least two stars.

## a. Answer each of the questions.

1. What is the Sun?

_______________________________________________

2. How many planets are there in our solar system?

_______________________________________________

3. Define an Orbit.

_______________________________________________

4. How many planets have their own natural satellite? Name them.

_______________________________________________

5. Which is a dwarf planet?

_______________________________________________

## b. Fill in the blanks with 'am', 'is' or 'are.'

My name _________ Meera. I _________ a girl. My teacher taught us about our Solar System. There _________ eight planets in our solar system. Pluto _________ a dwarf planet. The moon _________ a natural satellite.

c. Match the word links.

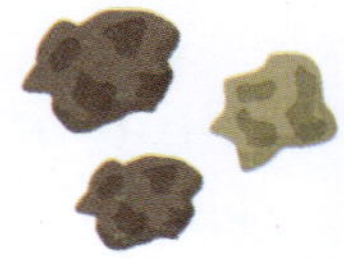

| | |
|---|---|
| Ma | une |
| Ven | on |
| Ea | ars |
| Mo | ury |
| Ura | n |
| Su | us |
| Sat | nus |
| Nept | uto |
| Jupi | rth |
| Pl | rs |
| Merc | ter |
| St | urn |

d. The word cards are not in order. Let's rearrange them to form meaningful sentences.

1. five | planet | the | dwarf | has | Pluto | moons

---

2. their | moons | around | planets | orbit | the

---

3. moons | Mercury | do | Venus | not | have | any | and

---

4. are | planets | there | in | eight | system | solar | our

---

5. Sun | a | rich | is | energy | source | of | electromagnetic

---

e. Can you find all the planets?

| U | R | A | N | U | S | Q | U | E | E | N | D |
|---|---|---|---|---|---|---|---|---|---|---|---|
| I | I | J | A | Y | P | D | U | C | L | E | V |
| T | T | D | H | O | N | E | Y | S | E | P | O |
| E | A | R | T | H | E | L | L | P | B | T | N |
| S | L | I | I | B | I | A | R | S | N | U | E |
| E | U | H | N | E | C | T | A | R | S | N | S |
| V | E | N | U | S | N | E | L | L | A | E | A |
| D | A | N | C | E | E | S | O | S | T | I | S |
| E | H | A | Z | K | U | M | L | Y | U | T | F |
| V | B | E | E | N | C | H | M | A | R | S | I |
| I | J | U | P | I | T | E | R | R | N | T | N |
| M | E | R | C | U | R | Y | A | M | E | Y | C |

MERCURY
VENUS
EARTH
MARS
JUPITER
SATURN
URANUS
NEPTUNE